M000309858

Samsara

Lauren Yee

A SAMUEL FRENCH ACTING EDITION

SAMUEL
FRENCH
FOUNDED 1830

SAMUELFRENCH.COM
SAMUELFRENCH-LONDON.CO.UK

ISBN 978-0-573-79997-6

www.SamuelFrench.com

www.SamuelFrench-London.co.uk

FOR PRODUCTION ENQUIRIES

UNITED STATES AND CANADA
Info@SamuelFrench.com
1-866-598-8449

UNITED KINGDOM AND EUROPE
Plays@SamuelFrench-London.co.uk
020-7255-4302

Each title is subject to availability from Samuel French, depending upon
country of performance. Please be aware that *SAMSARA* may not be
licensed by Samuel French in your territory. Professional and amateur
producers should contact the nearest Samuel French office or licensing
partner to verify availability.

MUSIC USE NOTE

Licensees are solely responsible for obtaining formal written permission from copyright owners to use copyrighted music in the performance of this play and are strongly cautioned to do so. If no such permission is obtained by the licensee, then the licensee must use only original music that the licensee owns and controls. Licensees are solely responsible and liable for all music clearances and shall indemnify the copyright owners of the play(s) and their licensing agent, Samuel French, against any costs, expenses, losses and liabilities arising from the use of music by licensees. Please contact the appropriate music licensing authority in your territory for the rights to any incidental music.

IMPORTANT BILLING AND CREDIT REQUIREMENTS

If you have obtained performance rights to this title, please refer to your licensing agreement for important billing and credit requirements.

SAMSARA received its world premiere at the Victory Gardens Theater (Chay Yew, Artistic Director) in Chicago, Illinois on February 13, 2015. The performance was directed by Seth Bockley, with sets by Joe Schermoly, costumes by Samantha C. Jones, lights by Sarah Hughes, sound by Nick Keenan, props by Jesse Gaffney, and dramaturgy by Isaac Gomez. The Production Stage Manager was Helen Lattyk, the Assistant Director was Laura Baker, and the Script Asistant was Carina Abbaticchio. The cast was as follows:

KATIE	Lori Myers
CRAIG	Joe Dempsey
SURAIYA	Arya Daire
AMIT	Behzad Dabu
FRENCHMAN	Jeff Parker

SAMSARA was developed by Victory Gardens Theater in Chicago, Illinois (Chay Yew, Artistic Director. Jan Kallish, Executive Director) as part of Ignition 2012, at the 2012 Bay Area Playwrights Festival, a program of the Playwrights Foundation (Amy L. Mueller, Artistic Director), and during a residency at the Eugene O'Neill Theater Center's National Playwrights Conference in 2013 (Preston Whiteway, Executive Director. Wendy C. Goldberg, Artistic Director).

SAMSARA was also developed at Desipina, the Exit Theatre, New Century Theatre Company, and the Playwrights' Center, with support from Theatre Bay Area and the Ludwig Vogelstein Foundation.

CHARACTERS

KATIE, 30s-40s, female, Caucasian

CRAIG, 30s-40s, male, Caucasian, her husband

SURAIYA, 18, female, Indian, their surrogate (also plays **BABY**)

AMIT, appears to be the same age as Suraiya, male, Indian, a fetus (also plays a **FATHER-TO-BE, INDIAN WOMAN IN LABOR, SURROGATE 1, MAILMAN, MOTHER**)

FRENCHMAN, any age, male, very French, a figment of Katie's imagination (also plays two **DOCTORS, SURROGATE 2**)

[Note: **BABY** and **MOTHER** speak in Gujarati. Also of the two **DOCTORS** in the play, the first is an American doctor and the second is a white British doctor living in India.]

SETTING

Northern California and western India.

TIME

The present.

PRODUCTION NOTES

Running time: 90 minutes, no intermission.

For a guide to pronunciation of Gujarati, French, and German, see the end of the play.

SPECIAL THANKS

Antje Oegel and Bailey Williams of AO International, Christina Augello, Snehal Desai, Naomi Iizuka, Pooja Patel, Aneesh Sheth, and Jayne Wenger.

For Adele Edling Shank

Scene

(CRAIG and KATIE's collective imagination.)

KATIE. *(to us)* With hundreds of thousands of babies being born across the every day, having a baby should be as easy as falling out of the sky.

> *(A FATHER-TO-BE waits in the center of the stage. KATIE watches him. Ding! A baby falls into his lap. He easily catches it. KATIE takes his spot, arms outstretched.)*

(to the sky) Right…?

> *(Ding! The baby falls somewhere else on stage. The FATHER-TO-BE catches this baby, too.)*

Shoot.

> *(KATIE moves to this new location, waits for the baby. CRAIG enters.)*

CRAIG. Catch anything?

KATIE. Not yet.

CRAIG. Don't worry, it'll come.

KATIE. Maybe if I stand over here…?

> *(KATIE stands in a new part of the stage, looks up, waits.)*

CRAIG. *(to us)* I think the early days were my favorite. I'd come home and she'd come home and before we could make dinner –

> *(KATIE jumps on CRAIG, they have sex.)*

KATIE. Oh God, again! Again!

CRAIG. Twice a day, even.

KATIE. I'm fertile for another four and a half hours!

(CRAIG finishes.)

CRAIG. How'd we do?

(KATIE has a negative pregnancy test.)

KATIE. Meh.

CRAIG. Again?

KATIE. Maybe we're not doing it right.

CRAIG. Maybe we're not doing it enough.

KATIE. A baby of our own: how hard could it be?

CRAIG. *(suggestive)* I don't know. Maybe we should find out.

(A little more sex. More sex. More sex. But KATIE still not pregnant.)

(to us) And eventually, we found the problem.

(An AMERICAN DOCTOR appears.)

DOCTOR. Uterine tumor. Very easy. Very easy to take care of.

(KATIE bursts into tears.)

CRAIG. See, honey? Very easy.

KATIE. That's not what he said.

CRAIG. It's not?

(Rewind.)

DOCTOR. Uterine tumor. Very easy. Very easy to take care of. No babies though. Definitely no.

CRAIG. Well, there's always adoption. *(joke)* Or a surrogate.

KATIE. A surrogate?

CRAIG. Your egg, my sperm, someone else's uterus.

KATIE. Craig, that's it!

CRAIG. That's what?

KATIE. We hire a surrogate.

CRAIG. You can't be serious. Are we serious?

KATIE. A baby of our own: how hard could it be?

CRAIG. We can think about it.

KATIE. Oh, Craig!

CRAIG. *(to us)* So we saved and saved and three years later…

> *(Fast forward to…)*

KATIE. Twenty thousand?!

CRAIG. That's good?

KATIE. That's it?!

CRAIG. That's not good. *(beat)* That's still good. For our income.

KATIE. We can't hire a surrogate for twenty thousand.

CRAIG. We could hire half a surrogate. Or a third of one.

KATIE. I don't want half a surrogate.

CRAIG. Then what do you want?

KATIE. I want –

> *(The sound of someone in labor. A scream.)*

I want –

> *(An online video of an* **INDIAN WOMAN IN LABOR***. Another scream.)*

CRAIG. You want to go to India?

> *(The* **INDIAN WOMAN IN LABOR** *screams louder.* **CRAIG** *winces. A vaguely* **BRITISH DOCTOR** *pulls a non-Indian* **BABY** *out of her.)*

KATIE. I found it online.

CRAIG. What *is* this?!

KATIE. My egg, your sperm, someone else's uterus!

DOCTOR. One hundred percent safe, one hundred percent natural!

> *(The* **INDIAN WOMAN IN LABOR** *groans, exhausted.)*

KATIE. This is exactly what we've been looking for!

CRAIG. But India?

KATIE. It's clean, it's comprehensive.

CRAIG. It's… far.

KATIE. It's cheap.

CRAIG. How cheap?

KATIE. I'm calling. I'm holding. I'm asking. We're in!

CRAIG. We're in what?

KATIE. They say if we want to secure our spot, we need to do it now!

CRAIG. Do what now?

KATIE. We go to a lab, we deposit our stuff, we get our results –

CRAIG. And?

KATIE. And if you're ready –

CRAIG. I am.

KATIE. We make the video, we choose a surrogate, we FedEx the… biological material to India. And in nine months, you bring it back.

CRAIG. *I* bring it back?

KATIE. Somebody needs to fly there.

CRAIG. Can't both of us need to fly there?

KATIE. It'll be cheaper without me.

CRAIG. It'll be scary without you. I hate traveling. I'll miss you.

KATIE. We'll talk every day. It'll be like I'm just in the next room.

CRAIG. But I miss you even *when* you're in the next room.

KATIE. You can do this. I know you can.

(*KATIE exits.*)

CRAIG. *(to us)* Picking a surrogate, it's a little like picking a horse.

(*We see into* **CRAIG**'s *mind:* **SURROGATES** *appear at a street corner, caress themselves provocatively.*)

SURROGATE 1. Hey, big boy.

SURROGATE 2. Hey, champ.

CRAIG. *(to us)* You send in your, material, and you get a catalogue, of all the possible recipients of your, material.

SURROGATE 1. You seen the stork lately?

SURROGATE 2. I'm real fertile tonight.

SURROGATE 1. My clitoris expands up to six times its size when aroused.

CRAIG. And it's up to you to, you know, pick. But Katie says that when you see the right one –

(A moment: CRAIG *sees a photograph of* SURAIYA.*)*

– you'll know.

(The SURROGATES *and* SURAIYA *disappear.* KATIE *enters with a guidebook.)*

KATIE. Eight months already.

CRAIG. Eight and a half. I wish you would get on the plane with me.

KATIE. I would if I could, but I can't. You know I can't.

CRAIG. But I wish you would.

KATIE. Just remember: we want this. We do.

*(*KATIE *hands the guidebook to* CRAIG, *exits.* CRAIG *closes his eyes, holds his breath. Blackout.)*

Scene

(One year ago – Video interview.)

KATIE. … hi. My name is Katie.

CRAIG. *(aside)* Katie…?

KATIE. Haber!

CRAIG. And Craig.

KATIE. Also Haber.

CRAIG. And we're the Habers!

KATIE. *(small)* Yay.

CRAIG. And this is our surrogate – surrogacy? –

KATIE. Surrogate –

CRAIG. – surrogate video! Welcome.

KATIE. And thank you for considering our application.

CRAIG. A little bit about us…

KATIE. Craig's a musician. He's got a band.

CRAIG. I'm the bassist. It's just me and my friends.

KATIE. They're kind of a big deal.

CRAIG. Among our friends. *(beat)* But my money job is construction.

KATIE. He also does bar mitzvahs!

CRAIG. And Katie…

KATIE. … works for a nonprofit. Mostly grantwriting. Boring. But enough of that! And on to –

(KATIE produces a set of questions.)

"When was the moment you decided to have children?"

CRAIG. Uh…

KATIE. *(leading)* "When was the moment…"

CRAIG. Oh! Um. Gosh.

KATIE. You remember!

CRAIG. *(no idea)* I mean, maybe.

KATIE. *(to camera)* Okay: so four, five years ago, we had this room –

CRAIG. *(realizes)* OH. Right. Yes. – four, five years ago we had this room –

> (**KATIE** *gestures vaguely behind her.*)

They can't see the room.

KATIE. Mainly for storage. And one day, I'm making breakfast and I'm looking for the egg beater, we got this egg beater for our wedding –

CRAIG. We're not big cooking people.

KATIE. And I'm looking everywhere, I'm looking in the closet, in the hall –

CRAIG. I'm asleep.

KATIE. Craig, he sleeps.

CRAIG. I do!

KATIE. And I get to the room and I don't know, I just take everything out of the office and I put it in the hallway.

CRAIG. She doesn't find the egg beater.

KATIE. And I'm about to ask Craig, you know, where's the egg beater?

CRAIG. I'm still sleeping.

KATIE. And I lean over –

CRAIG. – Saturday morning, first thing I hear –

KATIE. "I'm ready!" That's what I say.

CRAIG. And I'm like, is this an earthquake, did something happen?

KATIE. And I'm like, I think we should have a baby.

CRAIG. !!!

KATIE. I don't know what it was!

It's like this little voice –

It's like you're making French toast and suddenly this little voice –

And you know you're ready.

CRAIG. Katie hears voices. I hear Katie.

KATIE. *(small)* Yep.

Scene

(CRAIG's room.)

(CRAIG films his apartment in the clinic with his iPhone.)

CRAIG. So. Here we are. India. Living room. Couch, coffee maker. I didn't think they drank coffee in India, but I don't know, maybe that's for me. A/C: very important, if you want to keep from dying. My room, the bathroom – The toilet: the guidebook was wrong. It's the same as at home. Or maybe that's also for me…?

And the deck. So we can go outside without having to, actually, go outside. Looks out onto the McDonald's across the street, more buildings, the highway, the rest of Ahmedabad. They say Gandhi's house is around here, but knowing Gandhi, probably not that interesting. And out this window, we've got the rest of the clinic, the courtyard –

(Out the window, CRAIG sees a door to the courtyard open. SURAIYA sneaks out into the courtyard, with a book.)

– and the surrogate. Huh. We haven't met yet. Wonder what she's reading. *What to Expect When You're Expecting Someone Else's Child?*

(CRAIG is amused by his own joke, then remembers he's filming.)

But she looks good. Round.

(CRAIG swerves his camera back to himself.)

Anyway. Day two…of many. And that's Ahmedabad! Population six million… *(re: self)* And one. Soon to be two. Wish it were three.

Scene

(**KATIE**'s *living room.*)

(**KATIE** *sits at the coffee table with a box of old baby things. She rummages through, deciding what to keep/throw away. Maybe light frothy incidental music plays in the background.*)

(*Then a song starts. French music.* **KATIE** *looks up. The* **FRENCHMAN** *appears, magically playing an accordion with one hand and smokes with the other. He sings the last stanza of "Thank Heaven for Little Girls" from* Gigi.* *The phone rings. The* **FRENCHMAN** *keeps singing and gets close to* **KATIE**. *The phone rings again.* **KATIE** *sings the last line of the song with the* **FRENCHMAN**. *The phone rings a third time.* **KATIE** *answers.*)

KATIE. Craig!

CRAIG. Hey! How are you? What time is it there?

KATIE. One. In the morning.

CRAIG. Sorry. I keep thinking you're five hours behind.

KATIE. Nope! Fifteen.

(*The* **FRENCHMAN** *can be heard humming in the background.*)

CRAIG. What's that noise?

KATIE. Oh, it's the movie!

CRAIG. Which movie?

KATIE. The French movie. The one my mom and I used to watch all the time. I found the tape!

CRAIG. Really? Where?

---

*A license to produce *Samsara* does not include a performance license for "Thank Heaven for Little Girls." The publisher and author suggest that the licensee contact ASCAP or BMI to ascertain the rights holder to acquire permission for performance of this song. If permission is unattainable, the licensee should create an original composition in a similar style. For further information, please see music use note on page 3.

KATIE. With all my old baby stuff. It was in here all along! So now we can watch it together.

CRAIG. Do I have to?

KATIE. I don't mean you. I mean our daughter.

CRAIG. Or son.

KATIE. You wish. So you send me the new video?

CRAIG. Right. That. I am…almost about to send that to you right now.

KATIE. What've you been doing all day?

CRAIG. Sightseeing.

KATIE. Oh, so how's "AHMEDABAD?"

CRAIG. Well, it's a –

(**CRAIG** *consults his guidebook.*)

" – lively, fast-paced metropolis."

KATIE. Really?

CRAIG. Yes, though I've "found the pollution and noise to be somewhat stressful and off-putting."

KATIE. What'd you do?

CRAIG. I went to – "Sidi Saiyyed." Which is a mosque, apparently. It was "beautiful and pristine." I had a – "Indian sweets and chai following this." It was "good service, family-run."

KATIE. Craig, I have that same book.

CRAIG. You do?

KATIE. Have you gone anywhere since you landed?

CRAIG. Well, in order to do that, I'd have to cross the street first.

KATIE. It's been three days and you haven't even crossed the street?!

CRAIG. A very intimidating, very crowded street. No traffic lights, no crosswalks, all the cars just go whenever they feel like it, there's no way for you to cross! I stood there for ten minutes before I just went back in.

KATIE. What do all the other couples do?

CRAIG. I don't know. Because all the other couples –

KATIE. Yeah?

CRAIG. – they're couples.

KATIE. Eleven more days, okay? Try to enjoy yourself.

CRAIG. I will.

KATIE. One of us should have some fun before the baby comes. Blink and you miss it!

CRAIG. Sur-RYE-uh? Or Sur-RAY-uh?

KATIE. Did you ask her?

CRAIG. We haven't officially met.

KATIE. She was in that video you sent.

CRAIG. That's why I say "officially."

KATIE. You will. First checkup tomorrow. She's gotta be there, right?

CRAIG. I hope so. Whenever I ask the woman at the desk, she always says the surrogate's resting. I don't think she even knows which one I'm talking about.

KATIE. Poor baby.

CRAIG. I can't get to the McDonald's, the other couples are couples, and the internet takes forever to load. It's sooooo slow.

KATIE. Is it that slooooooow?

CRAIG. Yeeeeeeessssss, it is verrrrry sloooooooow –

> (CRAIG *makes a "power down" noise.* KATIE *does another version of this. Nice moment.*)

We should get off.

KATIE. Yeahhh.

CRAIG. And get some sleep.

KATIE. I will.

> (*They stay on the phone, making more robot noises.*)

CRAIG. Katie…

KATIE. It's just I keep having the craziest dream.

CRAIG. Of what?

KATIE. Of the baby. I see her…and she's Indian?

CRAIG. Indian?

KATIE. You're in a place and it changes you forever!

CRAIG. So India's going to rub off on her?

KATIE. Not that there's anything wrong with that! It's just, I wish I were there.

CRAIG. Me, too. Night, Katie.

> (CRAIG *hangs up.* KATIE *picks up the VHS tape.*)

FRENCHMAN. I thought you had to sleep.

KATIE. Just a little while longer.

FRENCHMAN. As you desire.

KATIE. You're a lot racier than I remember.

> (*The* FRENCHMAN *immediately sweeps her up in one hand, the cigarette still in the other.*)

And you're not really a smoker, right?

FRENCHMAN. *Moi?* I am just a figment of your imagination. I am just the product of baby frustration and your mother's unhealthy obsession with Maurice Chevalier.

KATIE. But are you tall?

FRENCHMAN. I am as tall as you want me to be.

KATIE. Are you beautiful?

FRENCHMAN. I am as beautiful as you want me to be.

KATIE. That's not very specific.

FRENCHMAN. I am as specific as you want me to be. I am *parfait!*

KATIE. Are you good at languages at least?

FRENCHMAN. But of course! But of course.

> (*The* FRENCHMAN *grabs, dips, kisses* KATIE. *She swoons, falls asleep. He checks to make sure she's asleep.*)

Sweet dreams. For now.

Scene

*(*KATIE*'s dream.)*

(A MAILMAN *appears.)*

MAILMAN. Mrs. Haber?

*(*KATIE *pops up from her sleeping position.)*

KATIE. Yes?!

MAILMAN. Special delivery. Seven pounds, eleven ounces.

KATIE. That's me!

MAILMAN. Sign for it.

> *(The* MAILMAN *hands* KATIE *a clipboard to sign, then cheerily hands* KATIE *a bundle from his bag. She pulls back the blanket, holds up a brown, ethnically incorrect baby.)*

KATIE. Um, excuse me?

MAILMAN. Yep?

KATIE. I think I might've gotten the, wrong, baby?

MAILMAN. Craig and Katherine Haber?

KATIE. Yes.

MAILMAN. Then she's yours!

KATIE. Yeah, but the babies in my family usually have… blue eyes. This baby's brown…eyed.

MAILMAN. Beautiful brown eyes. Congratulations!

> *(The* MAILMAN *exits.* CRAIG *enters.* KATIE *thrusts the baby at* CRAIG*.)*

KATIE. Craig! Look.

CRAIG. Oh, there she is. Knew I put her somewhere!

KATIE. No. *Look.* Doesn't something seem a little *off* to you?

CRAIG. What're you talking about? My nice brown skin, your pretty black hair. Healthy Indian baby.

KATIE. Why would we have a healthy Indian baby?

CRAIG. Oh, right.

KATIE. You sure you watched her come out?

CRAIG. Of course! Unless I didn't. Maybe it'll fade.

> (**CRAIG** *licks his thumb and rubs the baby's face.*
> *Nothing happens.*)

But this's gotta be our baby. See? *(re: tag on baby)* Last
name Haber, first name Madhulikadarshini.

KATIE. That's not a name.

CRAIG. It's the name on the tag. It's pretty.

KATIE. Madhulikadarshini.

CRAIG. In India, anyway. It means "princess" or "shit
demon." I don't know, we can google it.

KATIE. But I was gonna name her. I had a list.

CRAIG. Shame then. She already responds to
Madhulikadarshini. It'd be like trying to reprogram a
dog. *(whistles)* Here, girl. Here Madhulikadarshini.

> *(The baby seems to respond.)*

See? Like reprogramming a dog. Next one, dear.

KATIE. There may not be a next one!

CRAIG. Next dog, then!

KATIE. We don't have a dog.

CRAIG. Oh, come on, Katie. You have that attitude and you
won't enjoy any of this! Blink and you miss it.

KATIE. I guess. *(to baby)* And it's not gonna be like, years
from now, you're still gonna look –

> (**KATIE** *blinks. Fastforward to a grown baby, who*
> *still seems mentally on par with a five-year-old.*
> **CRAIG** *takes the* **BABY** *bundle from* **KATIE** *and*
> *replaces it with a wrapped present.*)

CRAIG. Happy birthday, Baby!

KATIE. Baby?

BABY. *Shukriya, bapuji.*[1]

KATIE. *(re: BABY)* Who is that?

CRAIG. That's Baby. Blink and you miss it! You didn't blink,
did you?

---

[1] Thank you, Father.

KATIE. Guess I must've. That was fast.

CRAIG. Yes, that was. Huh, Baby?

BABY. *Ha, juldi ghiyo.*[2]

CRAIG. Give Mommy a hug now.

> (**BABY** *reaches for* **CRAIG**.)

No, not me. Other mommy.

> (**BABY** *embraces the lamp.*)

BABY. *Ba!*[3]

CRAIG. Also wrong! *(to* **KATIE***)* Kids hug the darndest things! *(to* **BABY***)* Mommy, Baby. Mommy.

> (**BABY** *looks at* **KATIE**, *embraces* **KATIE**'s *present.*)

BABY. *(to the present) Ba…?*[4]

CRAIG. She'll learn. *(to* **BABY***)* You want to open your presents now or later?

BABY. *Pehla aapre jamile? Maane' bookh laaghiche.*[5]

CRAIG. All right then!

KATIE. *(whispers)* What did she say?

CRAIG. I don't know. I don't speak Indian.

KATIE. Indian?

CRAIG. Or maybe she's deaf. Have you tried signing to her?

BABY. *Maane ghoda nu bachu jove'!*[6]

CRAIG. *(simultaneously in sign language)* Hold your horses now, Baby. *(to* **KATIE***)* You should try, I think she understands.

BABY. *(to present) Hu thaane' prem karu chhu.*[7]

> (**BABY** *wanders out of the scene, hugging the present.*)

KATIE. How does she know Indian?

---

[2] Yes, that went by fast.

[3] Mommy!

[4] Mommy?

[5] First I want to eat. I'm so hungry.

[6] I want a pony!

[7] I love you, Mommy.

CRAIG. First few days: it's a formative time. You're in a place and it changes you forever.

(CRAIG *exits.*)

KATIE. Craig? Craig?

(*A noise. It throws* KATIE *from the dream. She wakes up. It's her cell phone alarm clock ringing. She silences it.*)

Silly, right? Silly.

Scene

(The clinic office.)

(CRAIG enters the room with his iPhone. He films.)

CRAIG. Day four. The clinic. *(turns, surprised)* And [mumbled version of SURAIYA]!

(SURAIYA sits prostrate in a chair, waiting for an ultrasound.)

Hey, I'm Craig by the way. I'm your father? *(stops)* Not YOUR father. Just THE father. *(tries again)* I'm the one that helped put that inside of you. So to speak. Hello. Nice to see you again.

SURAIYA. Again?

CRAIG. I saw you last night. Down in the courtyard.

SURAIYA. That must've been someone else.

CRAIG. Pretty sure.

SURAIYA. We all look alike.

CRAIG. Oh. Good to know. First time! If you couldn't tell.

SURAIYA. And where is your wife?

CRAIG. Home. America home.

SURAIYA. She's not coming?

CRAIG. Nope! Just me.

(The DOCTOR comes out. A vaguely British accent.)

DOCTOR. Sorry. "Dead baby on aisle five!" Joke. Well, not actually a joke, but uh – new day, new baby! *(beat)* I'll just get started.

CRAIG. Never thought I'd be standing in front of one of these.

DOCTOR. Well, sometimes you think you'll end up in Doctors Without Borders, and sometimes you just end up impregnating assorted Indian women. *(beat)* Sorry. Doctors Without Filters! All right: here we go!

(CRAIG *watches as the lights brighten to reveal*
AMIT. *He is a grown Indian man, the same age
as* SURAIYA, *even though he is in reality just an
amorphous blob.*)

DOCTOR. And…ohp. Ohp! There we go. There it is.

CRAIG. Wow. See that?

SURAIYA. Yes. "Wow."

(AMIT *gets up. Only* SURAIYA *sees him.*)

AMIT. Hi.

(SURAIYA *tries to ignore him.* AMIT *taps her on the
shoulder. She doesn't respond.* AMIT *taps harder.*)

SURAIYA. What.

AMIT. I said hi.

SURAIYA. I heard.

AMIT. Aaaaaand?

SURAIYA. And what?

AMIT. What do you say?

SURAIYA. *(relents)* Hi.

AMIT. What're they doing?

SURAIYA. They're looking at you.

AMIT. Yeah?

CRAIG. So can you tell the gender?

DOCTOR. You're not going to abort it, are you?

CRAIG. No…?

DOCTOR. Haha, joke. Haha, again not really: India.

CRAIG. What?

DOCTOR. *(slaps* CRAIG *on back)* It's a boy!

AMIT. I am a boy?

SURAIYA. *(unenthused)* You're a boy.

CRAIG. A boy!

(AMIT *magically sprouts male characteristics.*)

AMIT. I am a boy! *(beat)* What is a boy?

Scene

(Video interview.)

KATIE. *(reads card)* "Why a surrogate?"

CRAIG. What?

KATIE. *(re: card)* "Why a surrogate."

CRAIG. That's what my mom asks me all the time.

KATIE. *(playfully smacks CRAIG)* Craig!

CRAIG. Okay: so "why a surrogate?"

KATIE. Well, when Craig and I started looking, a surrogate just seemed to make so much sense. It just seemed natural.

CRAIG. "One hundred percent safe! One hundred percent natural!"

KATIE. We want someone to share our journey with.

CRAIG. Building a relationship that'll last forever!

KATIE. So to speak. That's what we care about.

CRAIG. Katie cares, which means I care, too.

KATIE. We do. Together.

(KATIE makes a passive aggressive/happy noise, they clutch hands to show unity.)

Scene

(The courtyard – Late at night.)

*(***SURAIYA*** *sits in an obscured part of the clinic's courtyard. She is surrounded by a stack of notes. The only light is from the glow of the moon.* **AMIT** *pokes at her.)*

AMIT. Hey. *Hey.*

SURAIYA. What.

AMIT. I am a fetus.

SURAIYA. Uh huh.

AMIT. And I will be born soon.

SURAIYA. Congratulations.

AMIT. I'm a fetus and I'll be born soon. *(gasps)* I can contract sentences!

SURAIYA. Everyone knows how to do that.

AMIT. Yeah, but I'm not even born yet. This means I'm a genius.

SURAIYA. Or it means *I'm* a genius. Maybe you're so smart because I'm so smart.

AMIT. What's the capital of Zimbabwe?

SURAIYA. What?

AMIT. What's the currency of Oman?

SURAIYA. Stop distracting me!

AMIT. Ha! I'm a genius! I'm a, a *WUNDERKIND*!

SURAIYA. Shhh!

AMIT. What?

SURAIYA. You're going to get us in trouble.

AMIT. But why would we be in trouble?

SURAIYA. Because it's lights out and if the auntie at the desk catches out me out here again, they'll take away our book, stick me back in that zoo with all those other women, and that'll be end of our studying.

AMIT. But why?

SURAIYA. Because I don't make the rules.

AMIT. But why?

SURAIYA. Because the exam's in thirty days, you're coming out in ten, and I'm not going to waste any more time not studying!

AMIT. Whoa. Relax. What could be so important?

SURAIYA. The entrance exam. For medical college.

AMIT. You want to be a doctor, like that reproductive imperalist? Be stuck here with desk auntie for the rest of your life?

SURAIYA. Oh, I'll become a doctor, but never an OBGYN. And not like him. I promise you that.

AMIT. You sound a little too sure of yourself.

SURAIYA. It's in my blood. And it's what my mother always wanted for me.

AMIT. She's a doctor?

SURAIYA. She was a nurse.

AMIT. That's not a doctor.

SURAIYA. But she could've been. That's why this is very important.

> (**AMIT** *sees a picture of something in the book.*)

AMIT. Whoa. Who is that freak?

SURAIYA. That's you, fetus.

AMIT. What?! Nooo. That thing's all pale and squishy, I'm not like that.

SURAIYA. Yes, you are.

AMIT. And I'm inside you?

SURAIYA. Yes.

AMIT. Seriously?!

> (**SURAIYA** *takes a stethoscope out and puts it on*
> **AMIT**. *He listens to her stomach.*)

Oooh, I can hear myself! *(to stomach)* Hello, meeee! Hellooooo! *(to* **SURAIYA***)* That is so weird.

SURAIYA. You're telling me.

AMIT. So you're my mother.

SURAIYA. I'm not your mother.

AMIT. Where is my mother then?

SURAIYA. In America. A land far, far away.

AMIT. When will I see her?

SURAIYA. Didn't you hear? She's not coming.

AMIT. But why?

SURAIYA. Don't ask me. Ask your father.

AMIT. Who?

SURAIYA. Him.

> (*Ding.* **CRAIG** *appears in* **SURAIYA**'s *mind, waves dorkily.*)

Your father.

AMIT. He can't be my father.

SURAIYA. Oh yes he is.

AMIT. But I don't even look like him! I look like you.

SURAIYA. (*shrugs*) In my imagination, all babies are brown.

AMIT. So if you're not the mother and you're not the father but I'm inside you –

SURAIYA. I'm just the holding tank. I keep you warm. Like a microwave.

AMIT. A "microwave."

SURAIYA. You put things in to make them warmer, and you take them out when they are done.

AMIT. That's what you're called.

SURAIYA. Yes.

AMIT. So Microwave, what's my name?

SURAIYA. I don't know.

AMIT. What's my name!

SURAIYA. You don't have a name.

AMIT. Everything has a name, Microwave. Fiji has a name. George Washington Carver has a name.

SURAIYA. Who?

AMIT. I want to know my name!

SURAIYA. You'll get a name when you come out.

AMIT. So can I come out now?

SURAIYA. No.

AMIT. How 'bout now?

SURAIYA. No.

AMIT. But it's so boring in here!

SURAIYA. You want to come out faster: grow faster.

AMIT. Really?

SURAIYA. Yep.

> (**AMIT** *concentrates. He grows a little.*)

AMIT. Oooh.

> (*He concentrates again. This time nothing happens.*)

This sucks.

> (**AMIT** *writhes in boredom.*)

SURAIYA. Stop, you little shithead: you're going to make both of us sick.

AMIT. What's a shithead?

SURAIYA. You.

AMIT. That's my name?

SURAIYA. *(beat)* Yes.

AMIT. I am Shithead.

SURAIYA. That's right.

AMIT. Wow.

Scene

(KATIE's *living room.*)

(KATIE *watches the French movie again. Next to her, the* FRENCHMAN *feeds her French foods. Romantic French music.*)

FRENCHMAN. *Croissant.*

KATIE. *Croissant.*

FRENCHMAN. *Macaron.*

KATIE. *Macaron.*

FRENCHMAN. *Bouef.*

(KATIE *makes a face: "bouef?"*)
  Bouef.

KATIE. *Bouef.*

(*A phone rings. She lowers the volume.*)

FRENCHMAN. *Pourquoi?*

(KATIE *grabs her cell phone.*)

KATIE. You are not here.

FRENCHMAN. But of course!

(KATIE *answers her phone.* CRAIG *is on the other end.*)

KATIE. Craig, how was it?

CRAIG. It's a boy!

KATIE. Who's a boy?

CRAIG. Our boy's…a boy!

KATIE. They told you?!

CRAIG. Yeah!

KATIE. Omigod. It's a boy!

(*The* FRENCHMAN *lights up a cigar in celebration, pops open a bottle of champagne.*)

FRENCHMAN. *C'est un garçon!*

(KATIE gestures for him to be quiet. He zips his lips, but hands her the champagne bottle. She drinks from it.)

KATIE. I thought we were not going to know.

CRAIG. I thought we were not going to know because we thought they weren't going to tell us...right?

KATIE. We talked about this.

CRAIG. Did we?

KATIE. We said we wanted to be surprised.

CRAIG. Well, we are. Ten days early, that's all. Sorry, I just got so excited, seeing him on that little screen for the first time. *(beat)* You're not disappointed, are you?

KATIE. No, I just kept dreaming about a her, is all.

CRAIG. Well, him now.

KATIE. *Au revoir, Amandine! Salut, Gerard.*

CRAIG. *Salut. (beat)* Also you're good at this: what do you think we should get her? The surrogate. I want to give her something.

KATIE. We are giving her something. We're giving her money.

CRAIG. Like something for her kid. Or kids.

KATIE. Don't get her anything. We don't want her thinking we're rich.

CRAIG. Yeah, like we went to India for a surrogate because we're rich.

KATIE. If she wants something, she can get it herself. She has the money.

CRAIG. Does she?

KATIE. She will, after this. People buy houses with the money they make.

CRAIG. The guidebook says Indians bond over food. Do you think that's true?

KATIE. You think they don't feed her?

CRAIG. I just don't want to go through this whole thing and still be a stranger to her.

KATIE. She's our surrogate. Not our life partner.

CRAIG. She kind of is, if you think about it.

KATIE. Now you sound like the people at work.

CRAIG. How is work?

KATIE. Meh. I hate them. I should quit. I even drafted an email.

CRAIG. Why quit, what quit?

KATIE. I never really wanted this job.

CRAIG. You always wanted to be a writer!

KATIE. Not a grant writer. I'm not going to actually send it.

CRAIG. Good!

KATIE. Though when my mom got pregnant, she quit.

CRAIG. Yeah, but you're not your mom.

KATIE. Excuse me?

CRAIG. I mean, WE'RE not your parents. Financially speaking. So don't try to be your mom.

KATIE. I'm not trying to be my mom. I'm just trying to think of what she might want for me.

CRAIG. Have a baby, right? Isn't that what this is for? Isn't that why I came all the way over here?

KATIE. No.

CRAIG. Shoot, my phone's dying.

KATIE. Just remember to send me the pictures! Craig, you hear me?

CRAIG. Call you later.

> (**CRAIG** *hangs up.* **KATIE** *takes a puff of the* **FRENCHMAN**'s *cigarette.*)

KATIE. Why doesn't this feel better?

FRENCHMAN. Eh?

KATIE. I am about to get everything I want. Why do I still feel like this?

FRENCHMAN. Because you are a greedy American who wants it all. You think having a baby will solve all your problems, distract you from your pathetic job, and bring you closer to your mother's memory. But it does not change the fact that you have married a man who is not enough.

KATIE. Why would I be with Craig, why would I send him to India if I think he's not enough?

FRENCHMAN. Because he is, how you say, your last ditch.

KATIE. He is not a ditch. And he's doing the best he can.

FRENCHMAN. You wanted a girl, he tells you it is a boy. Even though you have told him many times you want to be surprised. If he cannot remember that, what can he get right? It is just one part of the problem.

KATIE. What problem? There is no problem.

FRENCHMAN. But I am here. In your home. And when I am here, there is always a problem.

KATIE. I thought you were supposed to be a figment of MY imagination. A reflection of MY thoughts.

FRENCHMAN. And it is telling, is it not, that these are the things I say. What a dark little mind you have, *mon cherie.* And what is this about an email?

KATIE. I'm not actually going to quit –

FRENCHMAN. Quit! And the socialist safety net will catch you if you fall.

KATIE. That's more of a French / thing –

FRENCHMAN. Send it! How will you find out what your mother wanted for you?

(The FRENCHMAN *produces* KATIE*'s cell phone.)*

KATIE. You're kind of mouthy.

FRENCHMAN. I am French. I can be all mouth if you desire.

KATIE. And what do I desire?

FRENCHMAN. *C'est moi.*

KATIE. You are my mom's favorite movie, that's all.

FRENCHMAN. In a way, yes. In a way, I can be so much more if you will let me. Send it.

KATIE. Oh hell, why not!

*(*KATIE *sends the email. She kisses the* FRENCHMAN.*)*

KATIE. This means nothing.

FRENCHMAN. But of course! But of course.

(They make out. It turns into something raunchier.)

Scene

(The courtyard – Several nights later.)

(SURAIYA *is in the midst of telling* **AMIT** *a very long, very taxing bedtime story. He is almost asleep.)*

SURAIYA. And then Rama battled the demon king with his army of monkeys until at long last the demon king grew weary and took his leave…

*(***AMIT*** seems to be asleep.* **SURAIYA** *backs off.)*

…so Rama could finally get back to studying, so her life wouldn't be a complete failure and she wouldn't have to go back and live with her monkey cousins and be a millstone around her demon auntie's neck for the rest of her days.

*(***AMIT*** pops up again.)*

AMIT. And then what?! You didn't finish.

SURAIYA. And then Rama choked on his own sense of privilege and never woke up again.

AMIT. I'm hungry.

SURAIYA. Again? Are we seriously going through this every night?!

AMIT. But I am hungry every night.

SURAIYA. I thought you were tired.

AMIT. No, YOU were tired. I was awake. And now I am awake AND hungry.

SURAIYA. Well, it's lights out. No more food.

AMIT. Then we must get some!

SURAIYA. We are not going anywhere, Shithead.

AMIT. But you're my microwave, so you do what I say. Isn't that what they pay you for?

SURAIYA. The clinic? All they want is a – *(an ad)* "female in good health with a prior history of childbearing." As long as I don't screw this up, I'll earn "an easy five lakhs in just nine months!"

AMIT. "Five lakhs?"

SURAIYA. That's what they pay us.

AMIT. That's like, half a million rupees! That's like – *(beat, unimpressed)* eight thousand dollars.

SURAIYA. That's a lot of money.

AMIT. That's not even a car.

SURAIYA. It's enough.

AMIT. For what, a Vespa?

SURAIYA. Four years of medical college. They've already given me half and I get the other half when you come out.

AMIT. Yeah, but who knows when that will be.

SURAIYA. Oh, I know your due date. That sweet, sweet day. April thirtieth. Just eight more days.

AMIT. You don't know when I'm coming out. I come out when I say I'm coming out. In fact, maybe I'm coming out right now. Maybe I'm crowning as we speak.

SURAIYA. No, you're not.

AMIT. How would you know? You've never had a baby before.

SURAIYA. What're you talking about?

AMIT. Oh come on, we're all friends here. Admit it: no visitors, no stretch marks, you don't even know what a baby bjorn is.

SURAIYA. Fine! You're my first.

AMIT. First what?

SURAIYA. First baby.

AMIT. Ha! I knew it. *(beat)* Does the clinic know?

SURAIYA. I'm sure they could figure it out if they really wanted to.

AMIT. Probably will be disappointing when you do have children though, given that I am so amazing.

SURAIYA. Don't worry, Shithead. You're my first and my last.

AMIT. Ever?! But children are delightful! Just look at me!

SURAIYA. Hah. You are just a reminder of how terrible my life could've been if I'd ever gotten married.

AMIT. AND unmarried. Wow. Your life really will be wrecked if this doctor thing doesn't work out, huh? Being a girl sounds truly awful.

SURAIYA. At least I didn't have to worry about circumcision.

AMIT. Circum-what?

SURAIYA. What, you don't know about this? Americans, when you are a baby, they take your penis and they cut it off.

AMIT. The whole thing?!

SURAIYA. Or maybe just the skin.

AMIT. WHY WOULD THEY DO THAT?!

(A noise.)

SURAIYA. Someone's coming.

AMIT. I'M GOING TO BE SICK.

SURAIYA. Shhh!

(SURAIYA clamps a hand over AMIT's mouth, attempts to hide herself.)

(CRAIG appears with a bag of McDonald's.)

CRAIG. Oh, hey there! See? I knew it was you.

SURAIYA. I was just going to the bathroom.

(SURAIYA gathers up her things.)

CRAIG. Wait! I got you something.

AMIT. OHH. FOOD.

CRAIG. *(re: McDonald's bag)* I finally got to the McDonald's. Finally crossed the street! *(beat)* It's chicken!

AMIT. Get the burger! I need burger!

SURAIYA. Thank you, but I'm a vegetarian, I only eat –

AMIT. MEAT.

(AMIT begins to thrash. SURAIYA feels his movements. AMIT registers this. He raises a leg. SURAIYA moves.)

Wait a minute. I control you.

SURAIYA. *("no")* Mmm.

AMIT. *Yes.* And I'm hungry.

> (**AMIT** *puppeteers* **SURAIYA**. *She grabs the chicken burger, takes a huge bite.*)

SURAIYA. This is disgusting.

AMIT. And delicious.

> (**SURAIYA** *tries to put down the burger, but continues eating.*)

CRAIG. Gerard likes it, huh?

AMIT. Huh?

SURAIYA. Huh?

AMIT. Gerard?!

CRAIG. Amandine for a girl. Gerard for a boy. We like French stuff. *(corrects)* Katie likes French stuff.

SURAIYA. That's…nice.

AMIT. Don't encourage him!

SURAIYA. "Gerard."

AMIT. Shithead. Tell him I'm Shithead.

SURAIYA. Actually, that's a great name for a burger-eating American baby boy.

AMIT. Microwave. *Microwave.*

SURAIYA. Do you hear something?

CRAIG. No?

SURAIYA. Because I don't.

AMIT. You can't ignore me. You are my machine, you talk to me.

CRAIG. Can I touch him?

AMIT. No.

SURAIYA. Go ahead.

> (**CRAIG** *feels* **SURAIYA**'s *stomach.*)

AMIT. Get your Francophile hands off of us!

CRAIG. Hey, Gerard.

AMIT. *(sensitive/cranky)* Ow. OW.

CRAIG. Oh! He's awake. And – *strong.*

AMIT. Yeah, idiot: I'm thirty-seven weeks.

(A nice moment, before CRAIG *feels a small kick.)*

CRAIG. Ow!

SURAIYA. What.

CRAIG. Is he always so – feisty?

SURAIYA. He's probably just –

(AMIT *rocks around,* SURAIYA *stops, nauseous.)*

CRAIG. You okay?

AMIT. *(gleeful)* Nope!

(SURAIYA *throws down the rest of the burger.)*

CRAIG. Omigod, did I – ? You want me to get the woman at the desk?

SURAIYA. Please don't.

CRAIG. Are you sure? I can just –

SURAIYA. No! I'm not supposed to be out here.

CRAIG. But you're not doing anything wrong.

SURAIYA. *(more clearly)* I'm not supposed to be out here. I just need a –

(SURAIYA *doubles over.)*

CRAIG. I... I...am going to be right back.

(CRAIG *hurries off stage.)*

Scene

(Outside/KATIE's living room.)

(KATIE wakes up, half-covered by a blanket. Morning. The living room is in disarray. Maybe her underwear is somewhere it should not be. Maybe she knocks into some empty champagne bottles. What happened here last night? Her phone rings. She answers.)

CRAIG. Katie –

KATIE. Heyyy! Craig! Heyyy!

CRAIG. I can't do this.

KATIE. Do what?

CRAIG. I want to come home. I can't do this by myself.

KATIE. Yes, you can.

CRAIG. If you were here, you'd know what to do. If you were here, you could fix this.

KATIE. Fix what?

CRAIG. I think I'm lost.

KATIE. Is that all?

CRAIG. I was looking for the store, I started walking, and now I think there is a goat following me.

KATIE. You bring a map?

CRAIG. I should've taken a map.

KATIE. You'll find it.

CRAIG. How?

KATIE. Remember when we were in Ensenada and we were trying to find that restaurant? You were the one who found it! You remember how you did that?

CRAIG. No.

KATIE. You looked at me and you said, "I just followed the light."

CRAIG. "Just follow the light."

KATIE. You're going to be fine, Craig. You are enough.

CRAIG. I'm a what?

KATIE. You are enough.

CRAIG. Katie, I can't [no signal].[8]

KATIE. Craig, what?

CRAIG. I said, I can't [no signal].

KATIE. Craig, you're breaking up.

CRAIG. Okay, that goat is definitely [no signal].

> (**CRAIG** *hangs up. Then he sees a light, he follows it.* **KATIE** *begins to clean up the champagne bottles. The* **FRENCHMAN** *bursts from out of nowhere, maybe in a dressing gown, coffee in hand.*)

FRENCHMAN. *Allo.*

KATIE. Aaaah!

FRENCHMAN. You are awake. At last!

> (*The* **FRENCHMAN** *grabs a tote bag full of French baby toys, dumps the toys on to the coffee table.*)

KATIE. What is all this?

FRENCHMAN. These are the toys for the *bébé*. Now that we are in this together!

> (*The* **FRENCHMAN** *begins to demonstrate one of the toys.*)

KATIE. I should…get to work.

FRENCHMAN. But you have quit! Remember last night? The email.

KATIE. Omigod, the email! Why did I do that? Why did *you* let me do that?!

FRENCHMAN. You do not want the job. Why would you not quit?

KATIE. I can't quit. I've got a baby coming.

---

[8] **KATIE**, I can't **hear you**.

I can't **hear you**.

Okay, that goat is definitely **following** me.

FRENCHMAN. You will rely on the state to get by. Take a break from your 35-hour work week. And in this way, you will get what you want.

KATIE. This is not France! This is America! People over here don't get what they want! I don't have time to fuck around.

FRENCHMAN. That is not what you said last night. *(beat)* Or do you remember nothing of our torrid affair?

KATIE. What affair? No affair. How can this be an affair if you're not even real? Omigod, this movie is ruining my life.

> (*The* FRENCHMAN *tries to complete the romantic embrace.* KATIE *kills this moment.*)

You should go.

FRENCHMAN. *Sacre bleu,* you are breaking up with *moi?*

KATIE. I don't need you anymore.

FRENCHMAN. But you have invited me into your life. Into your baby's life. And once you invite the Frenchman in, you will never be rid of him.

KATIE. You are insane. And dangerous.

FRENCHMAN. And you are bringing a child into this world with a man you find inadequate and a surrogate you refuse to face.

KATIE. Okay, that's it.

> (KATIE *finds the VHS, takes it out of the case.*)

FRENCHMAN. What are you doing?

KATIE. I am getting rid of you. Permanently.

FRENCHMAN. But that is your mother's. You destroy that, you destroy her memory, all those times you had together. You would not dispose of me so easily.

KATIE. We'll see about that.

> (KATIE *crushes the VHS. The* FRENCHMAN *dies a protracted, sad death. Sad dramatic but maybe still romantic music.*)

Omigod!

(Finally, the **FRENCHMAN** *dies.)*

I'm sorry, but it had to be done!

*(***KATIE*** exits. The* **FRENCHMAN** *pops back to life.)*

FRENCHMAN. Hon hon hon hon!

Scene

(The courtyard – Hours later.)

(AMIT reads from a letter. SURAIYA weakly enters.)

SURAIYA. All right, carnivore, let's go to sleep.

AMIT. Not yet.

(SURAIYA notices AMIT holding the letter.)

SURAIYA. You found the letter. Great.

AMIT. What is a whore?

SURAIYA. Not tonight, Shithead.

AMIT. Your auntie calls you a "whore." What is that?

SURAIYA. It's someone who…sells their body for money.

AMIT. And that's you?

SURAIYA. According to her. But joke's on her, because I didn't sell, I only rented!

AMIT. So can I be a whore?

SURAIYA. No.

AMIT. You're a whore. I want to be a whore, too!

SURAIYA. It's not a good word.

AMIT. It's not?

SURAIYA. It is a terrible word. It is the worst thing you can call someone.

AMIT. *(re: letter)* Then why do you keep this?

SURAIYA. As a reminder.

AMIT. Of what?

SURAIYA. Of why I can never go back to my auntie's house.

AMIT. What about your parents? Won't they miss you?

SURAIYA. My parents are dead.

AMIT. What's "dead?"

SURAIYA. Oh boy.

AMIT. What is it?

SURAIYA. It means…you go on a very long, very fun vacation!

AMIT. That's it?

SURAIYA. ... where you fall asleep and you never wake up again. That is dead.

AMIT. And this happened to parents?

SURAIYA. It happens to everyone.

AMIT. Even you?

SURAIYA. In time.

AMIT. But not me, right?

SURAIYA. Not for a very long time, Shithead.

AMIT. How long?

SURAIYA. I don't really know. None of us do.

AMIT. And this doesn't alarm you? To walk around each day, with no idea if it's perhaps your last?

SURAIYA. It's part of the deal.

AMIT. Then I'm not coming out.

SURAIYA. Everyone has to come out sooner or later, Shithead.

AMIT. Then I'll come out later.

SURAIYA. Seven days and you won't have a choice.

AMIT. Please don't make me come out. I come out, I have to live. I come out, I have to grow and I have to die. Please don't let me die.

SURAIYA. You're not going to die!

AMIT. Promise?

SURAIYA. And if you do, you'll go through *samsara*!

AMIT. *Samsara?*

SURAIYA. The cycle we all go through. We're born, we live, we die, we're born, we live, we die. We come back as something else, forever and ever.

AMIT. But what if I come back as a trash can? Or a waffle?

SURAIYA. You won't. And if you do, you won't remember anything from before anyway.

AMIT. Not even you?!

SURAIYA. No.

AMIT. Not even if I try really, really hard?

SURAIYA. You're going to have a very good life, Shithead. And one day this will just be a story your parents tell you. About what it was like before you were born.

AMIT. But I don't want to forget. Tell me I won't forget. Microwave?!

SURAIYA. You're not going to forget.

AMIT. And that I'll be protected forever.

SURAIYA. You will.

AMIT. And you'll be the one to do that?

SURAIYA. Maybe?

AMIT. "Maybe?!"

SURAIYA. Fine. Yes.

AMIT. But how will I remember that?

(SURAIYA *leans in, kisses* AMIT *on the forehead.*)

SURAIYA. There. See? Now you will never forget.

(CRAIG *stands in the doorway with a plastic bag and a Starbucks drink.*)

CRAIG. So how're you feeling?

SURAIYA. Better.

CRAIG. I got you some medicine.

(CRAIG *dumps the contents of his bag on the table.*)

I got you all the medicine, actually. I didn't know which one you'd need, so I got all of it. Which I now see might've been a mistake.

SURAIYA. Which one is which?

CRAIG. Well! This one's if you've got a headache.

This one's for the runs.

This one's if your menstrual blood is spotty and unheroic.

– that's a direct quote –

These are digestive biscuits. They seemed tasty.

(CRAIG *takes a biscuit out of the box, eats one.*)

(re: last medicine) And I'm not sure what this one is.

SURAIYA. This is an antacid. This is what I needed.

CRAIG. Really?

SURAIYA. See? You did get the right one.

CRAIG. I did, didn't I? Buy out the whole store and you're bound to get one right.

> *(**SURAIYA** takes an antacid tablet.)*

Did you feel like this last time?

SURAIYA. Hm?

CRAIG. Last time you were pregnant.

SURAIYA. Oh. Yes?

CRAIG. How many kids do you have?

SURAIYA. One. One boy.

CRAIG. What's his name?

SURAIYA. *(thinks)* Shithe…ed.

CRAIG. Shaheed?

SURAIYA. Yes. Shaheed.

CRAIG. You must miss him.

SURAIYA. Eh.

CRAIG. You sure Gerard'll be okay for tonight?

SURAIYA. He's fine.

CRAIG. You sure?

SURAIYA. Here –

> *(**SURAIYA** takes out her stethoscope.)*

Just listen.

> *(**SURAIYA** holds the stethoscope against her stomach, **CRAIG** listens.)*

AMIT. Hello?

CRAIG. I can hear him.

> *(**AMIT** turns and hears **CRAIG**, who hums. **AMIT** hears him humming and hums the tune, too. They share a musical moment. Maybe this is also reflected in mirrored body language.)*

Ohhh, weird.

SURAIYA. See? He's fine.

CRAIG. Do all the surrogates get one of these?

SURAIYA. It was my mother's. She was a nurse.

(**SURAIYA** *puts away the stethoscope.*)

CRAIG. Well, I hope you feel better. *(tries)* And Suraiya?

SURAIYA. *(nods)* Suraiya.

(**CRAIG** *leaves his lantern with* **SURAIYA,** *wanders back to his room in darkness.* **SURAIYA** *continues studying.*)

Scene

(Video interview.)

KATIE. "Our favorite place!"

CRAIG. … is?

KATIE. No, that's the question.

CRAIG. Oh. Here, I guess.

KATIE. Or France!

CRAIG. She's never been and that's her favorite place!

KATIE. So?

CRAIG. Katie is obsessed with French things.

KATIE. *(to CRAIG)* I am / not! *(to camera)* I am not.

CRAIG. You are. You are! She is. She's obsessed.

KATIE. My mother's side is French.

CRAIG. French Canadian.

KATIE. That's French.

CRAIG. That's French Canadian.

KATIE. My family's from *Montreal.*

CRAIG. Not that we've been.

KATIE. We're homebodies. We don't really travel.

CRAIG. She's never flown in a plane.

KATIE. I can't!

CRAIG. She's afraid.

KATIE. I am not!

CRAIG. Katie doesn't like planes and I don't like traveling. So we're a pair!

KATIE. It's more than that.

CRAIG. Okayyyy –

> (CRAIG *waits for* KATIE *to tell the story. She doesn't. So he does.)*

So when Katie was twelve –

KATIE. No.

CRAIG. When Katie was twelve –

KATIE. I was ten. And no.

CRAIG. Lemme just say –

KATIE. Craig –

CRAIG. Lemme just say – / so when Katie was ten –

KATIE. Craig

Craig

CRAIG.

> *(**CRAIG** stops.)*

There is no story.

> *(Beat. Then **CRAIG** to the camera – .)*

CRAIG. When Katie was ten, she didn't like flying anymore. The end.

Scene

(The clinic office – The next day.)

(Once again, **SURAIYA** *in the chair,* **CRAIG** *on his iPhone.)*

(The **DOCTOR** *enters with blood on his hands/ white coat.* **CRAIG** *wanders back into view.)*

DOCTOR. Sorry! Had to squeeze in another delivery before lunch. So how're we feeling? Heard we had some trouble last night.

SURAIYA. No.

CRAIG. Trouble? No. No trouble. What trouble?

DOCTOR. Let's take a look.

(The **DOCTOR** *operates the sonogram machine.)*

Well, he's big.

AMIT. Of course.

DOCTOR. He's strong.

AMIT. Naturally.

DOCTOR. And he's got his head in the right direction. Which is good enough for me! In fact, I'd say we're ready.

CRAIG. For what.

DOCTOR. The delivery!

AMIT. Delivery?

CRAIG. I thought that was next week.

DOCTOR. You've lucked out. There's been a cancellation, so we can move the c-section up to tomorrow!

CRAIG. What does that mean?

DOCTOR. It means you could be going home with the baby a week early.

AMIT. WHAT?!

CRAIG. Isn't this kind of fast?

DOCTOR. Miracle of life! Can't be stopped. You and your wife DID preapprove it on your application.

CRAIG. We did?

DOCTOR. But if you'd prefer to give up the spot...

AMIT. Give up the spot, give up the spot,

CRAIG. And Suraiya, she'd get to go home, too?

DOCTOR. Once we're done, the surrogate'll be back home
    before she knows what hit her.

CRAIG. What do you think, Suraiya?

AMIT. Microwave, no. Microwave, please.

SURAIYA. I...think we should all go home.

CRAIG. Okay. Let's go home.

DOCTOR. Righto! We'll slice this bugger out in no time!
    (beat) Which is actually exactly how it works. Very
    speedy procedure. *(to* CRAIG*)* You won't feel a thing.
    Until tomorrow!

> *(The* DOCTOR *exits.)*

CRAIG. Tomorrow I will be a father.

> *(A silence as they both let this news sink in.*
> SURAIYA *pokes* AMIT, *who seems deep in thought.)*

SURAIYA. Shithead?

AMIT. Yes?

SURAIYA. You're going to be fine.

AMIT. I know.

SURAIYA. You do?

AMIT. I will find a way. I *will* see you again.

SURAIYA. Of course you will.

> *(Beat.)*

CRAIG. Sooo. Last night: what're you going to do?

SURAIYA. Sit. Read. Pack.

CRAIG. Really?! Last night: nothing.

SURAIYA. Where would I go?

CRAIG. Out.

SURAIYA. I haven't really gone out much since I got here.

CRAIG. Not even to the McDonald's?

SURAIYA. We're not allowed.

CRAIG. Then we should definitely go out, celebrate.

SURAIYA. "We?"

(CRAIG *takes out a wad of rupees.*)

CRAIG. Yeah, "we." Otherwise I'll have to blow all these rupees at the airport.

SURAIYA. But desk auntie's not gonna let me –

CRAIG. Who?

SURAIYA. The woman at the desk.

CRAIG. That lady must be ninety-four years old. She's not gonna stop us. Gerard should see the city before he goes. See where he's from.

SURAIYA. He should. But shouldn't we let the doctor know?

CRAIG. About what? You heard him: "tomorrow." C'mon! Last night in "AHMEDABAD!"

(CRAIG *and* SURAIYA *exit, just a little bit giddy.*)

Scene

(KATIE's living room.)

*(KATIE's phone sits on the coffee table, alone.
KATIE'S VOICEMAIL starts.)*

KATIE'S VOICEMAIL. Hi, I'm not here right now.

Because I'm probably showering or sleeping or doing
the two or three things that take me away from this
phone.

But if you're Craig and you're calling and it's three a.m.
over here, please call back as soon as humanly possible.

Really.

Whenever.

As many times as you need!

*(Beep. CRAIG leaves a message. He goes in and
out.)*

CRAIG. Hey!

Guess what.

They moved up the due date!

It's tomorrow, so I'm going to [no signal] with [no
signal]

So we can [no signal]

I think my reception is [no signal]

Which I know is going to drive you absolutely [no
signal],

But [no signal] call me! [9]

*(Lights out over CRAIG. KATIE enters, runs to her
phone.)*

KATIE. Oh shit shit shit shit.

---

[9] It's tomorrow, so I'm going to **go out** with **SURAIYA**.
So we can **celebrate**.
I think my reception is **kind of going in and out**,
Which I know is going to drive you absolutely **crazy**,
But if there's **anything, just call me**!

(**KATIE** *immediately dials* **CRAIG**. *Lights up on*
CRAIG'S VOICEMAIL.)

CRAIG'S VOICEMAIL. Hello – !

KATIE. Craig?

CRAIG'S VOICEMAIL. I'm not here right now.

(**KATIE** *redials several times*.)

Or now.

Or now!

Because I'm somewhere else, as decisions are being
made, babies are being born –

KATIE. Really?

CRAIG'S VOICEMAIL. Not yet. *(considers)* Though who knows!
But if you leave a message –

KATIE. I don't want to leave a message.

CRAIG'S VOICEMAIL. I'll talk to you later.

KATIE. I don't want to talk to you later.

CRAIG'S VOICEMAIL. Beep.

KATIE. Craig, it's me. It's four a.m. over here. Call me
before I –

(**BABY** *appears suddenly in her living room*.)

– fall back asleep. Shoot.

(**KATIE** *is sucked into her dream. She tries to teach*
BABY *English*.)

Cat. Cat?

BABY. *Chal? Chal?*[10]

(**KATIE** *cries,* **BABY** *pats* **KATIE** *on the back*.)

Chalse, chalse. Hu koshish kharti chhu.[11]

(**CRAIG** *enters*.)

CRAIG. Baby learn anything yet?

KATIE. No.

---

[10] Come? Come?
[11] It's all right. You are trying.

CRAIG. Don't worry: it'll come. *(to* **BABY**, *also in sign language) Ja, kleine?* [12]

KATIE. She doesn't speak German, Craig. Or sign language.

CRAIG. Never know if you don't try.

> *(Doorbell)*

> *(exiting) Ich komme!* [13]

KATIE. *(tries to sign)* You'd tell me if you were deaf, right?

> **(CRAIG** *enters with* **MOTHER**, *played by* **AMIT**.*)*

CRAIG. Look who I found, Baby: your mother!

BABY. *Ba!* [14]

> **(MOTHER** *and* **BABY** *embrace.)*

CRAIG. He's come to claim her.

KATIE. But I'm the mother. I'm the *ba*. That *ba* can't be a mother. That mother's a man.

CRAIG. I know, right? *(shrugs)* India. Ready, Baby?

KATIE. Craig, no!

CRAIG. We always knew it was just a matter of time, Katie.

MOTHER. *Thaane Bharat gumsei. Tya loco tene heran nai kare'.* [15]

KATIE. No! Stop that – *(bats* **MOTHER** *away)* No *ba*. No India.

CRAIG. Katie.

KATIE. Baby's not ready. Baby's still a baby.

CRAIG. Time flies. Say your goodbyes now.

KATIE. Well, Baby, there were some things I was going to tell you. For when you learned English. Or when I understood Indian. But anyway –

> **(KATIE** *takes out a list.)*

"Um, number one: Be kind to your elders.

---

[12] Yes, child?

[13] I'm coming!

[14] Mother!

[15] You will like India. There people will not bother you.

KATIE. *(cont.)* Stop running around, you're going to fall and hurt yourself.

Take that out of your mouth. That's dirty."

*(**MOTHER** gestures "wrap it up".)*

CRAIG. Katie, they've gotta go. *Mach schnell!*[16]

*(**KATIE** skips to the end of list.)*

KATIE. "Don't sleep with strange men.

Never have sex without a condom.

And there is no substitute for actually being there."

CRAIG. All right. *(also in sign language) Es ist an der Zeit zu gehen, ja?*[17] *Ja. Kuss Mami auf Wiedersehen.*[18] Say *"auf Wiedersehen,"* Katie.

KATIE. *Auf wiedersehen.*

CRAIG. In sign language. So she'll understand.

KATIE. *(also in sign language) Auf Wiedersehen...?*

*(**MOTHER** picks up **BABY** and exits with her over his shoulder. She waves to **KATIE** and **CRAIG** as she exits.)*

BABY. *Owjo! Owjo!*[19]

KATIE. Do you think we'll ever see her again?

CRAIG. Probably not. But as they say, *"So ist das Leben!"*[20]

---

[16] Shake a leg!
[17] It is time to go, yes?
[18] Kiss Mommy goodbye.
[19] Goodbye! Goodbye!
[20] Such is life!

Scene

(Outside.)

*(**SURAIYA** stands outside a mall with her Starbucks drink. Things/people/animals whizz by.)*

AMIT. And that?

SURAIYA. Is a parking lot.

AMIT. And that?

SURAIYA. Is two people holding hands.

AMIT. And that?

SURAIYA. Is an Armani Exchange.

AMIT. "An Armani Exchange."

SURAIYA. You're going to see all this in America.

AMIT. But it won't be the same! Take a picture, take a picture.

SURAIYA. Your father'll be back with the phone in a minute.

AMIT. Oh right, we'd better hurry then.

*(**AMIT** takes out lipstick, tries to put it on **SURAIYA**.)*

SURAIYA. What is that?

AMIT. It's lipstick!

SURAIYA. Where did you get that from?

AMIT. You're the one who stopped in the Sephora.

SURAIYA. You're supposed to pay for that.

AMIT. I'll learn that lesson later. Now come here. Don't worry. It's your color. I've already tried it.

SURAIYA. What're you doing?

AMIT. I am improving upon your looks.

SURAIYA. Why?

AMIT. There is this thing called "looove." And when someone has it for another, they will do anything that person says! So if we can acquire some looove from the American, he will bring you home with us and my plan will be complete!

SURAIYA. That's not how love works, Shithead.

AMIT. "Amit."

SURAIYA. What?

AMIT. My name is Amit. It means "infinite." I think this is a good name for me. I looked up "shithead." Not as flattering.

(CRAIG *enters from the mall.*)

CRAIG. The toilet in the mall? It is not the same. Anyway, on to Sidi Saiyyed! This way?

SURAIYA. I think so. I've only been there once.

CRAIG. You're not from here?

SURAIYA. I'm from Surat. It's a couple hours south. We're famous for our diamonds.

CRAIG. Okay then, Suraiya from Surat, we'll just…follow the light.

(CRAIG *picks a direction. They walk in that direction.*)

Are you excited for tomorrow? Or (*checks time*) basically today!

SURAIYA. You mean for the cesarean?

CRAIG. I mean Shaheed. Seeing him again!

SURAIYA. Oh. Yes. Shaheed.

CRAIG. You must miss him, huh?

SURAIYA. He…can be a little shithead sometimes.

AMIT. You know it.

SURAIYA. But he constantly surprises me.

(*They approach a building.*)

Sidi Saiyyed.

CRAIG. That's it? Kind of small.

SURAIYA. Look closer.

(*They get closer. Sidi Saiyyed's intricate windows come into view.*)

AMIT. Wow.

CRAIG. Look at those windows.

SURAIYA. All the latticework is made of stone.

CRAIG. Wonder what happened to that window.

SURAIYA. The British took it.

CRAIG. Like they just ripped it out of the wall?

SURAIYA. Basically, yes.

CRAIG. Sidi Saiyyed. What do you think that means?

SURAIYA. It's the name of the man who built it.

CRAIG. He was a king?

SURAIYA. He was a slave.

CRAIG. How do you know all this?

SURAIYA. You visit Ahmedabad, you have to see Sidi Saiyyed. My father took me here a long time ago.

CRAIG. Have they come out to see you while you've been here?

SURAIYA. My parents are dead.

CRAIG. Oh. Sorry to hear.

SURAIYA. It was a long time ago. And *samsara*, right?

CRAIG. *Samsara?*

SURAIYA. The cycle of life. Nothing ever goes away. It just gets reborn somewhere else. At least that's what my mother told me.

CRAIG. Stand there. In front of the first one.

(SURAIYA *poses with* AMIT. CRAIG *takes a picture.*)

Nice.

SURAIYA. Let me see.

(*The iPhone freezes.*)

CRAIG. Hold on. It's an old phone. I can just email it to you. What's your email?

SURAIYA. …

CRAIG. Sorry, that's weird.

SURAIYA. It's not.

CRAIG. You don't have to say.

SURAIYA. No, it's uh – Here.

> (SURAIYA *types in her email.*)

CRAIG. Thank you.

SURAIYA. For what?

CRAIG. For doing this. 'Cause it is a big thing for us. We won't forget this. And we won't let him forget. Gerard will know where he comes from.

SURAIYA. You mean India?

CRAIG. Yeah, maybe! Yeah, he'll know India. And you!

SURAIYA. But you wouldn't bring him here. Not for a while.

CRAIG. No, but maybe. Or you could come visit us!

AMIT. Sure!

SURAIYA. You're not serious.

CRAIG. Yeah! Why not!

SURAIYA. How?

AMIT. Who cares!

CRAIG. Well, get on a plane, fly into SFO, and, uh –

> (CRAIG *takes a flimsy plastic card out of his wallet.*)

– get on the BART!

SURAIYA. The what.

AMIT. The BART.

CRAIG. Bay Area Rapid Transit. You get out, you get on the BART, and you get off at Colma. And that's where we'll be. Easy.

> (CRAIG *hands the BART ticket to* SURAIYA. AMIT *squeals.*)

SURAIYA. You actually want me to come?

CRAIG. … yeah! Not now. Later, maybe.

AMIT. Or now.

CRAIG. When we save enough. Or you could email. Or skype. Something. I just want you to exist for him, I guess.

(SURAIYA holds on to the BART ticket.)

It's got twelve-fifty on there now. So: don't lose it.

SURAIYA. You're going to be a good father.

CRAIG. I hope so.

SURAIYA. If your wife is as excited about the baby as you are –

CRAIG. Ha. Katie would love to hear you say that.

SURAIYA. Pardon?

CRAIG. Katie has been looking forward to this for *forever*. FOR-EV-ER. Whereas, I never saw myself with kids.

SURAIYA. Really?

CRAIG. It just seemed like a lot of work, creating something that would probably just blame you for everything later in life.

SURAIYA. So what changed?

CRAIG. I met Katie. And everything changed.

SURAIYA. But she's not here.

CRAIG. Flying's not really her thing.

SURAIYA. How can she want this as much as you do if she's not here?

CRAIG. She really does want to be here. It's just, when she was ten –

SURAIYA. Yes?

CRAIG. When she was ten, uh – Here, hold on.

> *(CRAIG takes out his phone, finds a video.* **SURAIYA** *and* **AMIT** *lean over* **CRAIG***'s shoulder.* **CRAIG** *presses play.)*

Scene

(Video interview.)

KATIE. So… When I was ten, my parents went skiing in Montreal. They went to Montreal *to* ski. And they were in this commuter jet, like every seat's a window or an aisle, small – And they crashed and – That was kind of how my mother died. – her luggage was fine, though! So weird! – But, uh, no, I don't like flying. And spiders! I hate spiders. There was this one time, at Thanksgiving, Craig and I, we were at his mom's and there was this spider – big old spider, huge – and so I grabbed the turkey pan. And I smashed it. And I felt pretty good about that. I'm not afraid of spiders, I just don't do spiders.

Scene

(The courtyard – Very late at night.)

(CRAIG stumbles in with a sleeping SURAIYA in his arms. An awake but sleepy AMIT follows.)

(CRAIG's phone rings. CRAIG puts SURAIYA down, AMIT snuggles next to her.)

(CRAIG answers.)

CRAIG. Katie.

KATIE. Where is she?!

CRAIG. What?

KATIE. The surrogate, where is she?

CRAIG. Suraiya? She's right here.

KATIE. She's with you?

CRAIG. Yeah. She's fine.

KATIE. OMIGOD, WHERE WERE YOU?

(CRAIG moves away, to not wake SURAIYA.)

CRAIG. Out. We went out.

KATIE. That's it?

CRAIG. Yeah. We got Starbucks and a *thali*. You ever had a *thali?*

KATIE. I don't fucking care what a *thali* is.

CRAIG. I left you a message. Did you call me back?

KATIE. YES.

CRAIG. Sorry, my reception sucks whenever I leave the clinic.

KATIE. Then why did you leave in the first place?

CRAIG. We were celebrating.

KATIE. You celebrate when you GET a baby. You do not celebrate the fact that your surrogate could give birth at any moment? Why didn't you tell anyone you were leaving?

CRAIG. I thought I waved at desk auntie when we left.

KATIE. How could you be so irresponsible?

CRAIG. Sorry, I didn't realize it'd piss you off so much.

KATIE. I'm not pissed off, Craig. It's just, how would you feel if you got a frantic call from the clinic: "Hey, your surrogate is gone, we don't know where she is, AND we can't get a hold of your husband?"

CRAIG. If they'd called me, I'd know you could handle it. I'd trust you.

KATIE. And if something happened to the baby?

CRAIG. What's going to happen? Someone steals the baby?

KATIE. The surrogate steals the baby?

CRAIG. Suraiya would never do that.

KATIE. I don't know, okay? I don't know her. I don't know this clinic. I have no idea what's going on over there. You haven't emailed me anything in three days. I don't even know what our baby looks like. It's like I'm not even there!

CRAIG. Because you aren't!

KATIE. What do you want me to do about it?

CRAIG. Get on a plane and ACTUALLY be here? And ACTUALLY see?

KATIE. You know that's just not possible.

CRAIG. Why didn't you come?

KATIE. *Because I can't.*

CRAIG. Sure, getting on a plane, I know why it scares you, I know why you can't. I'm asking: why didn't you?

KATIE. You know why.

CRAIG. Fine, but remember: you are missing this. And for the rest of your life, for the rest of the baby's life, you will have not been here. Because you have chosen not to be here. And there is no way I can fix that for you.

KATIE. Okay, new plan. Do you know what're you going to do for the rest of the trip?

CRAIG. Get the baby. I know.

KATIE. No. You are going to be on the phone with me every hour on the hour from now until you get on the plane with our freaking baby. Because until you come home, I do not want you to ask yourself "What Would Katie Do?" I want you to ask ME, directly, what you should do.

CRAIG. That's ridiculous. I'm not doing that.

KATIE. Yes, you will.

CRAIG. But it won't be enough. It's never enough! And you know why? Because it's just not the same. So you know what? No more.

KATIE. No more what?

CRAIG. No more emails. No more pictures. No more phone calls. You wanted this, not me.

KATIE. That's not true. Craig, you know that's not true.

CRAIG. You want to see what's happening, get on a plane and see for yourself.

KATIE. Craig, please –

CRAIG. Bye, Katie.

> (CRAIG *hangs up, puts his phone on silent. Lights out over* KATIE. *He puts his phone down next to the still sleeping* SURAIYA, *then goes out for a walk. As soon as* CRAIG *is gone,* AMIT *opens one eye, then another. He opens* CRAIG*'s phone. He clicks on a video.*)

(*voice over*) Okay, so: "why a surrogate?"

AMIT. Ooh.

Scene

(Video interview.)

KATIE. Well, when Craig and I started looking, a surrogate just seemed to make so much sense. It just seemed natural.

CRAIG. "One hundred percent safe! One hundred percent natural!"

KATIE. We want someone to share our journey with.

CRAIG. Building a relationship that'll last forever!

KATIE. So to speak. That's what we care about.

CRAIG. Katie cares, which means I care, too.

KATIE. We do. Together.

> (KATIE *makes a passive aggressive/happy noise, they clutch hands to show unity. A moment and then they break recording.*)

That was too much.

CRAIG. That was fine. You think they won't want our money?

KATIE. I want a good surrogate.

CRAIG. We pay them, they work for us. Ten to one, the surrogate doesn't even see any of this. I mean, she's the one whoring herself out, telling people – *(stops)* What DO they tell people?

KATIE. Nothing, probably. I mean, what do you say?

CRAIG. *(bad Indian accent)* "It appears your mother got gangraped by a pair of crazy Americans and their sperm donor."

KATIE. You are so BAD, Craig.

CRAIG. So this thing between the four of us, not a gangbang?

KATIE. I prefer "group effort."

CRAIG. What do you think India'll be like?

KATIE. You're a guy. You'll be fine. In India, it's the women they treat like dirt.

CRAIG. Eeeugh.

KATIE. Also: I think he's French.

CRAIG. Who?

KATIE. The sperm donor. When the woman from the clinic called, I asked her, "What's he like, did we get the good stuff?" you know what she said?

CRAIG. What?

KATIE. "*Oui.*"

CRAIG. "*Oui.*"

KATIE. We asked for "European male." That's not completely crazy.

CRAIG. *(gives in)* That is not completely crazy.

KATIE. She has their profiles, she knows where they're from. Why else would she say that?

CRAIG. I think she was messing with you.

KATIE. Fine then, what do you think he is, the sperm donor?

CRAIG. I…haven't really thought about it.

KATIE. At all?!

CRAIG. All I care about is healthy. You give me healthy and he could be Ted Kaczynski for all I care.

KATIE. Oh don't say that! Do not say that!

CRAIG. Ted Kaczynski: European male.

(KATIE *notices the camera.*)

KATIE. Shoot. Camera.

CRAIG. Is it still running?

KATIE. I think so.

CRAIG. I'll edit it out when I put it all together.

KATIE. Delete this.

CRAIG. I can edit it out!

KATIE. Delete this. Or I will send it to your mother.

CRAIG. Okay. Later. I'll do it later.

Scene

(The clinic courtyard – Before sunrise.)

(SURAIYA, who now holds the phone, pauses the video. CRAIG enters.)

CRAIG. Happy due date! You ready?

(No response.)

Suraiya?

SURAIYA. No. Not really.

CRAIG. Is it nerves?

SURAIYA. No. You.

CRAIG. What?

(SURAIYA hands the phone back to CRAIG.)

Oh hey, you found my phone! I've been looking everywhere for that –

SURAIYA. How could you say that about me?!

CRAIG. Were you looking at my videos? Because that wasn't for you.

SURAIYA. Right. Because I'm a whore.

CRAIG. Jesus, I didn't mean YOU.

SURAIYA. You meant someone like me. Who does what I do.

CRAIG. YES.

SURAIYA. Who also got gangraped by you and your wife.

CRAIG. It was a joke. From MONTHS before I met you.

SURAIYA. And your French sperm donor?

CRAIG. I'm sorry, did you need to know about him, too? Katie can't carry babies. And I can't make 'em.

SURAIYA. So does it make me more or less of a whore, this being my first?

CRAIG. First surrogacy?

SURAIYA. First Baby.

CRAIG. Total. But what about Shaheed?

SURAIYA. There is no Shaheed.

CRAIG. There is no Shaheed. Of course! Of course the surrogate *I* chose has never done this before! Katie will love this. "100% safe! 100% not a total shitshow!"

SURAIYA. This is funny to you?

CRAIG. You don't think so?

SURAIYA. I think it's sad. It makes me feel sorry for you.

CRAIG. Join the club.

> (SURAIYA *flicks the BART ticket onto the floor, exits. The* FRENCHMAN *enters out of the shadows.*)

FRENCHMAN. *Allo.*

CRAIG. Who's there?

FRENCHMAN. He who has always been on your mind.

CRAIG. I don't think about you.

FRENCHMAN. Of course you do! I would. Wonder about the kind of man your wife has chosen.

CRAIG. She didn't choose you.

FRENCHMAN. Oh no?

CRAIG. What's there to choose? She knows nothing about you. You could be anyone. You could be a pedophile, a criminal, a serial rapist.

FRENCHMAN. *(another distinctive but non-French accent)* I may not even be French.

CRAIG. Exactly! *(to* FRENCHMAN*)* And your health history. Cancer, liver problems –

FRENCHMAN. Consumption, gout –

CRAIG. Syphilis.

FRENCHMAN. *C'est possible!*

CRAIG. Any number of things you could've omitted. So none of this means anything –

FRENCHMAN. Except that he is my child.

CRAIG. Yes.

FRENCHMAN. And my child will know this because you will have told him.

CRAIG. I bet you aren't even French.

FRENCHMAN. But of course, you will never know for sure.

(The FRENCHMAN *disappears.)*

Scene

(The clinic courtyard.)

*(**AMIT** enters in a cat burglar outfit with a suitcase.)*

AMIT. Microwave, there you are! We must go.

SURAIYA. We should talk.

AMIT. Yes! But first we must hightail it out of here.

SURAIYA. To where?

AMIT. There is a medical college in Mumbai across the street from a day care. All we have to do is bust out of here, get some clever moustaches, find ourselves an elephant –

SURAIYA. But what about desk auntie?

AMIT. That woman could not stop a wheel of cheese.

SURAIYA. There's your father.

AMIT. That idiot?

SURAIYA. And then there's me.

AMIT. What about you?

SURAIYA. *(deliberately)* I don't want you. I can't.

AMIT. So you're giving me up to those people?

SURAIYA. Those people are your parents.

AMIT. But I don't want them. I want you. Suraiya. Suraiya from Surat. I choose you.

SURAIYA. You're not any part of me.

AMIT. You're my blood, my lungs. How can I not be a part of you?

SURAIYA. I don't have that many choices.

AMIT. But they're going to cut you open! Take me out!

SURAIYA. And maybe that's what I want, too.

AMIT. You know that's not true.

SURAIYA. You won't remember any of this. I promise. And one day this will become just a story I tell myself about something that happened a long time ago.

AMIT. You can't pretend this never happened.

SURAIYA. I have to. Soon, you're going to be gone. So I need to stop thinking about you. And I think I should start now.

AMIT. This is crap. This is, this is – *bullshit.*

SURAIYA. Goodbye, Shithead. You're going to have a wonderful life.

> *(Lights out on* **SURAIYA**. *She is still there, but something has changed. From* **AMIT**'*s perspective, she is now dim, removed.)*

AMIT. Microwave. *Microwave. (beat)* I know you can hear me! You can hear me, right? Microwave? Microwave!

> *(But his words seem to echo in some great abyss.)*

Scene

(**KATIE**'s *living room.*)

(*The* **FRENCHMAN** *sits at the coffee table with a pipette and sets of Petri dishes. The living room has been transformed into the* **FRENCHMAN**'s *living room. French flags, croissants, cheese platters dot the room. A French bulldog slobbers in the corner.* **KATIE** *enters.*)

FRENCHMAN. *Allo, mon chou.*

KATIE. What're you doing here? I got rid of you.

FRENCHMAN. Yes, you imagine I am imaginary, that I have no bearing on the world as it is. And I like to remind you that I am not.

KATIE. You're not real.

FRENCHMAN. But I am a real person. Who has given your child life. And that is very real. *(beat)* You ask me for this great thing, you get what you want and then it is: "*Au revoir, Français! Merci et au revoir!*" That is not so kind either, *n'est-ce pas?*

KATIE. You were supposed to be anonymous. I bought an anonymous sperm donor.

FRENCHMAN. You know nothing about me, my occupation, my interests, my *raison d'etre.* You do not even know my name.

KATIE. No.

FRENCHMAN. And in my country, that is anonymous. Now move, your large and infertile form is blocking the sun from my eyes.

KATIE. *(re: Petri dishes)* What are those?

FRENCHMAN. Those are my eggs.

KATIE. You mean my eggs?!

FRENCHMAN. You have many eggs. These are just the eggs of yours that are mine. From when we traded.

KATIE. We did not trade.

FRENCHMAN. You think I give without getting?

You think I am stupid as the moon?

You think: "Look at the Frenchman: he is round and stupid and faraway as a moon! Hon hon hon hon!"

Non, non.

You wanted a French baby because it would be disdainful of others, *oui?*

Now: I want an American baby so it will develop strong capitalistic urges and a laughably high self-esteem.

> (**KATIE** *plucks a contract from the* **FRENCHMAN**'s *pile.*)

KATIE. You signed a contract. *(reads)* "Section 34, Item 16a: sperm donor hereby relinquishes all rights to implanted embryos, now and forever."

FRENCHMAN. And the next item?

> (**KATIE** *looks down at the contract.*)

KATIE. "Section 34, Item 16 … b: egg donor, in turn, hereby grants all unused eggs to sperm donor, now and forever, hon hon hon." *(beat)* That was really small print.

FRENCHMAN. All things start small, and they grow bigger. *(re: Petri dish)* They will grow bigger.

KATIE. Well, I am taking them back.

> (**KATIE** *takes the Petri dish.*)

There. I've taken them back.

FRENCHMAN. Except for the others.

KATIE. "Ze others?"

FRENCHMAN. *(re: embryos)* Those were just some of the some of your eggs.

KATIE. Some of the some?

FRENCHMAN. Most of the some of your eggs are now floating about the world in ways we cannot control. We have implanted them in Spain! In Romania! Even in that sons of bitches country England! Do not worry: they will know nothing of you.

KATIE. Frenchman, you can't!

FRENCHMAN. I do not understand why you are so angry, *mon cherie.* You and me, what we are doing, we are the same.

KATIE. We are not the same.

FRENCHMAN. Perhaps you are right.

> (*The* FRENCHMAN *snatches the Petri dish back from* KATIE, *holds it up.*)

For I see this for what it truly is. And you do not. But here, you may have this woof woof instead.

> (*The* FRENCHMAN *picks up the French bulldog, hands it to* KATIE.)

And in this way, we both get what we deserve.

KATIE. This is not what I want. I don't WANT a woof woof!

FRENCHMAN. I did not say what you want. I said what you deserve.

KATIE. I want a baby. I DESERVE my baby.

FRENCHMAN. You Americans: you want and you want, and in doing so, you forget –

KATIE. What?

FRENCHMAN. That sometimes there are things beyond your control. Such as this.

> (*The* FRENCHMAN *conjures up an image. A shadow of* AMIT *somewhere.*)

KATIE. Who is that?

FRENCHMAN. Someone you could have known. *Au revoir.*

> (*The* FRENCHMAN *smugly takes his Petri dish, exits.*)

Scene

(Somewhere – Dawn.)

(In the moment between darkness and light, **AMIT** *stands at the door of the clinic. The sound of the world just beginning to wake up. He ninjas through the empty streets, until he is very, very far away. He comes to a great opening in the earth.)*

*(***AMIT*** stands at the very edge of it. The ground shakes a little. He looks left, looks right, and then he jumps. A faint noise and then nothing.)*

Scene

(The clinic courtyard the next morning.)

*(**SURAIYA** watches the sun rise. **CRAIG** enters, they don't look at each other.)*

CRAIG. Morning.

SURAIYA. Morning.

*(**CRAIG** stares at **SURAIYA**.)*

CRAIG. Suraiya.

SURAIYA. What.

CRAIG. Where's the baby?

SURAIYA. Huh?

*(**SURAIYA** looks down. She's no longer pregnant, or at least does not appear to be.)*

Amit? Amit!

Scene

(The clinic.)

DOCTOR. … on the bright side: she'll be perfectly fine. She keeps what we've already paid her, you get your final payment back, all shipshape. Just, you know, no baby.

(A dazed CRAIG *says nothing.)*

Mr. Haber? Can you hear me? We lost the baby.

CRAIG. We lost the baby.

DOCTOR. Right.

CRAIG. So where is he?

DOCTOR. Who?

CRAIG. The baby.

DOCTOR. Let's try this again.

CRAIG. Why aren't we looking? We should be looking. What kind of place is this, you're just losing babies left and right?!

DOCTOR. Mr. Haber, I think you need to sit down.

CRAIG. No, I'm not going to sit down.

DOCTOR. Maybe you should call your wife.

CRAIG. No.

DOCTOR. Where're you going?

CRAIG. I'm going to find my baby.

DOCTOR. Mr. Haber, we lost the baby.

CRAIG. Yes, and if you lost him, I can find him.

*(*CRAIG *exits.)*

Scene

(Outside – Twilight.)

*(**CRAIG** wanders through a dark field. **SURAIYA** enters.)*

CRAIG. Gerard? Gerard?

SURAIYA. Craig, you need to go back inside.

CRAIG. Not until I find the baby.

SURAIYA. He's gone. We lost him.

CRAIG. But nothing ever goes away. It just goes somewhere else. That's what you said, right? So if we lost him, we can get him back. He just needs to know that we're out here, waiting for him.

SURAIYA. You should go home.

CRAIG. How can I go home? How can I leave without my baby? How can I live the rest of my life without my baby?

SURAIYA. I don't know, but I'm leaving.

CRAIG. For home?

SURAIYA. No.

CRAIG. Then for what?

SURAIYA. The rest of my life.

CRAIG. But how can you live the rest of your life if we don't find him?

SURAIYA. Because I have to. Because I'm going to pass the test, I'm going to become a doctor, and I'm going to be the person my mother always wanted me to be.

CRAIG. How can you be so sure?

SURAIYA. Because it's what was meant to be.

CRAIG. Gerard. Gerard?

SURAIYA. His name wasn't Gerard. Or Shaheed.

*(**CRAIG** walks off.)*

It was Amit. It means infinite.

*(**SURAIYA** looks out into the space. It is vast. She looks for some sign of **AMIT**.)*

*(**KATIE** calls **CRAIG**. The phone rings and rings.)*

Scene

(**CRAIG** and **KATIE**'s collective imagination.)

(**CRAIG**'s phone rings, he ignores it. **KATIE** comes into view.)

KATIE. Craig. Your phone is ringing. Answer your phone.

CRAIG. It's gonna be you.

KATIE. I know it's gonna be me.

CRAIG. I answer that phone and it's going to be real. I answer that phone and all this will come true.

KATIE. Something's wrong, I know it.

CRAIG. Then why don't you call the clinic? Ask them.

KATIE. I don't want to hear it from them. I want to hear it from you.

CRAIG. Won't change anything.

KATIE. I know. But tell me anyway. Can you do that?

CRAIG. Yeah.

(**CRAIG** answers his phone. He tells **KATIE** everything. Instead of words, we hear what **KATIE** hears: the buzz of the lamp, the hum of the refrigerator, the house settling, the living room, the kitchen, the upstairs, the office, the crib in the office –)

KATIE. Oh.

CRAIG. Oh?

KATIE. I wish I was there.

CRAIG. No, you don't.

KATIE. I do. I wish I was there. Or you were here. Everything comes out wrong over the phone.

CRAIG. I wish we were in the same room at least. You ever notice that? Even at home, I'd walk into a room and I'd see you, receding into the next one.

KATIE. You buy a house, it has rooms in it. You're liable to end up in different places.

CRAIG. Is that what you want for us?

KATIE. No.

CRAIG. Then what do you want?

KATIE. What do *you* want?

CRAIG. I… I want to build things. I want to build things with you. You think we still can do that?

KATIE. I hope so.

CRAIG. Yeah?

KATIE. Yeah. *(beat)* I'm at the airport. I bought a ticket.

CRAIG. You should stay home.

KATIE. It's non-refundable.

CRAIG. Oh. *(beat)* You're not going to like it here.

KATIE. That's okay.

CRAIG. So you're coming?

KATIE. We're boarding. We're leaving. We're taxiing. I'm here.

CRAIG. Where?

KATIE. You don't see me?

CRAIG. No?

KATIE. I see you.

CRAIG. Where?

KATIE. Turn around.

(CRAIG *does.* KATIE *is there.*)

CRAIG. Oh. Didn't see you there. *(beat)* How was your flight?

KATIE. Fine. It was, fine.

CRAIG. Good.

KATIE. Wow. It is hot.

CRAIG. A hundred and three.

KATIE. So what do we do now?

CRAIG. Well, the car's across the street.

(KATIE *looks at the busy, sprawling street in front of them.*)

KATIE. This street?

CRAIG. Yep.

KATIE. Jeez.

CRAIG. Told you. You ready?

KATIE. Uh huh.

CRAIG. You sure?

      *(**KATIE** grabs **CRAIG**'s hand.)*

KATIE. Let's go.

      (They take a first step into a vast empty space.)

      (Curtain.)

GUJARATI PRONUNCIATION GUIDE

Special thanks to Pooja Patel and Aneesh Sheth

"Shukriya, bapuji" – *Shook-reeya baa-poo-jee*

"Ha, juldi ghiyo" – *Haa(n), jaldee guy-o* (the "n" is a nasal sound but not pronounced)

"Pehla aapre jamile? Maane' bookh laaghich." – *Pay-lah aap-rey jameelay? Munay* boook laa-gay-ch.* (the "u" sound in "Munay" and here after are pronounced as a shwa vowel)

"Maane ghoda nu bachu jove'!" – *Munay go-daa noo bachoo jo-vay!*

"Hu thaane' prem karu chhu." – *Hoo(n) thunay pray-m karoo choo.*

"Chal? Chal?" – *Chul? Chul?*

"Chalse, chalse. Hu koshish kharti chhu." – *Chaal-say, Chaal-say, Hoo(n) ko-sheesh karthee choo.*

"Thaane Bharat gumsei. Tya loco tene heran nai kare'." – *Thu-nay Bhaarat gum-say. Tya(n) loco thunay 'ay-raan naa kare.*

"Owjo! Owjo!" – *Ow-joe! Ow-joe!*

GERMAN PRONUCIATION GUIDE

Special thanks to Isaac Gomez

"Ja, kleine?" – *Ya, KLINE-eh?* (last syllable is grace note)

"Ich komme!" – *Ichhh* (almost a hiss), *COHMa*

"Mach schnell!" – *Mahk SCHNELL!*

"Es ist an der Zeit zu gehen, ja? Ja. Kuss Mami auf Wiedersehen."

– Ess ist ahn dare zite tzu GAY-en, ya? Ya. Cous Mami awf VEE-der-tzehn.

"ein braves Mädchen." – *ine BRAH-vess MAID-chen*

"So ist das Leben!" – *Zo ist dahs LEH-ben!*

FRENCH PRONUNCIATION GUIDE

Special thanks to Isaac Gomez

"Parfait" – *Pahr-FAYE*

"Moi?" – *Mwah?*

"Au revoir." – *Oh rev-wah*

"Croissant" – *CWAH-sohn* (the n is nearly silent)

"Macaron" – *MA-ca-rohn* ("ma" and "ca" have the same vowel sound as "map," not "mop")

"Bouef" – *Beuff* (the vowel is closer to "deux" than the American "buff")

"Pourquoi?" – *Pore kwah?*

"C'est un garçon?" – *Say oon GEHR-sohn* (the n at the end of "un" and the "r" and "n" in "garçon" is nearly silent)

"Non?" – *Nohn?* (the second n is nearly silent)

"Au revoir, Amandine! Salut, Gerard." – *Oh rev-WAH, Ah-moh-DEEN! Sa–LOO, Zhe-rahr.*

"bébé" – behbeh

"oui" – wee

"Sacre bleu" – *SAH-cruh bleuh* (the vowel in "blue" is closer to "deux" than "bluh")

"C'est la vie" – *Say la vee*

"Mon cherie" – *mohn share-REE*

"Mon chou" – *mohn SHOO* (the n at the end of "mon" is nearly silent)

"Hon hon hon" – *Hohn Hohn Hohn* (the n is nearly silent)

"C'est possible!" – *Say poh-see-bluh* (last syllable of "possible" is a grace note)

"Français!" – *FRAHW-say*

"Merci et" – *MEHR-see eh*

"n'estce pas?" – *ness pa?*

"raison d'etre" – *RAY-zohn DEHT-ruh* (the n at the end of "raison" is nearly silent, as is the second syllable of "d'etre")

"n'est-ce pas?" – *nes pah?*

"Mon cochon" – *mohn KO-shohn* (final n's of both words are nearly silent)